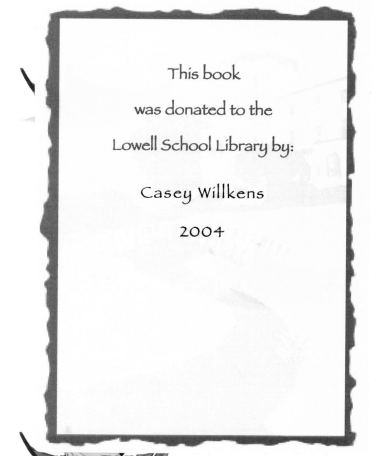

This book

was donated to the

Lowell School Library by:

Casey Willkens

2004

For Grace —E. L.
For my mum, Joan —L. P.

Published by
PEACHTREE PUBLISHERS, LTD.
1700 Chattahoochee Avenue
Atlanta, Georgia 30318-2112
www.peachtree-online.com

ISBN 1-56145-305-6

First published by Oxford University Press in Great Britain, 2003

10 9 8 7 6 5 4 3 2 1
First Edition

Library of Congress Cataloging-in-Publication Data:

Laird, Elizabeth.
Beautiful bananas / written by Elizabeth Laird ; illustrated by Liz Pichon.-- 1st ed.
    p. cm.
  Summary: On her way to her grandfather's house with a bunch of bananas, Beatrice has
a series of mishaps with jungle animals who each substitute something new for what
she is carrying.
  ISBN 1-56145-305-6
[1. Jungle animals--Fiction. 2. Gifts--Fiction.] I. Pichon, Liz, ill. II. Title.
PZ7.L1579 Be 2004
[E]--dc22   2003016661

Beautiful Bananas

Elizabeth Laird

Illustrated by Liz Pichon

PEACHTREE
ATLANTA

"Goodbye, Mama," says Beatrice. She's on her way to see her granddad. She's got a present for him. It's a beautiful bunch of bananas.

On the way, she meets a giraffe, who flicks his tufty tail. He whisks the bananas right off Beatrice's head, and they land with a splash in the stream.

"Oh, I'm sorry," says the
giraffe. He picks some flowers
and bends down low to give them
to Beatrice.

"My granddad will like these,"
she says.

A swarm of bees settles on the flowers. "Hey!" Beatrice cries. She beats the bees off, but the flowers are crushed and spoiled.

"We're very sorry," say the bees.
They wrap up some honeycomb and
give it to Beatrice instead. On she goes,
down the path.

Some naughty monkeys see the honeycomb. "We like honey!" they cry. They snatch it away from Beatrice. All the honey drips onto the ground.

"Stop!" says Beatrice. "That honey was for my granddad."

"Oh dear," say the monkeys. They run up into the trees and pick some mangoes for her instead.

Beatrice takes
the mangoes
and hurries on.

Suddenly, out jumps a lion! "Aaghh!" screams
Beatrice. She's very, very scared. She drops the
mangoes, and they all roll away.

"Don't be scared," says the lion. "I didn't mean to frighten you." He pulls out one of his whiskers and gives it to her. Beatrice runs on, holding the whisker in her hand.

A parrot sees the whisker. He thinks it's a twig. He swoops down and carries it off to build his nest. "Come back!" shouts Beatrice. "That whisker is for my granddad!"

"My mistake," squawks the parrot. He pulls a long feather out of his tail and gives it to Beatrice. On she goes again.

But what's that long gray thing dangling down beside the path? Beatrice brushes it with her feather.

"You're ti-ti-tickling me!" gasps the elephant.
"Ah-choo!" His sneeze blows the feather away.

The elephant is sorry. He stretches out his trunk and picks a bunch of bananas for Beatrice. She claps her hands. "Oh, thank you," she says. "Bananas are best, after all."

Here at last is Granddad's house, and here at last is Granddad. "I've got something for you," says Beatrice, and she gives him his present—a beautiful bunch of bananas!